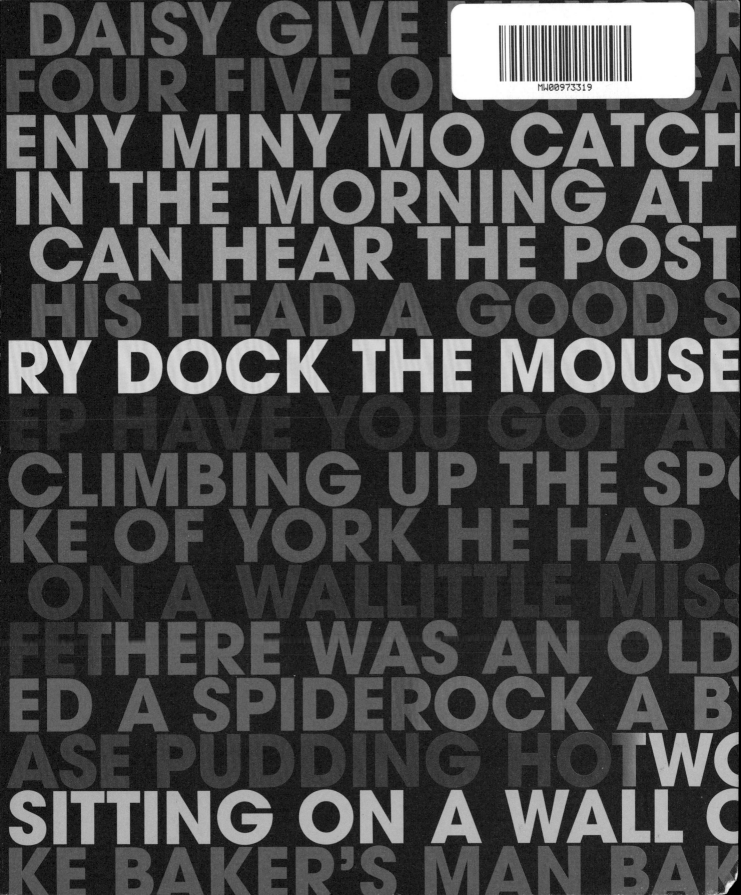

Some other titles by PatrickGeorge:

   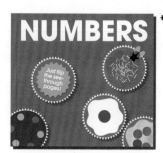

* Due out in February 2012

© PatrickGeorge 2009
First edition published in 2009
Second edition revised published in 2011

Illustrated, designed and published by
PatrickGeorge
46 Vale Square
Ramsgate
Kent CT11 9DA
United Kingdom

www.patrickgeorge.biz

ISBN 978-0-9562558-6-0

British Library Cataloguing in Publication Data.
A catalogue record for this book is available from the British Library.

Printed in China.

Little Miss Muffet
and other rhymes

Getcha rhyme on, Baby G!
xoxo,
ANNA

One, two, three, four, five.
Once I caught a fish alive,
Six, seven, eight, nine, ten,
Then I let it go again.
Why did you let it go?
Because it bit my finger so.
Which finger did it bite?
This little finger on my right.

The Grizzly Bear
is huge and wild,
He has devoured
the infant child,
The infant child
is not aware
He has been eaten
by the bear

Daisy, Daisy give me your answer do.
I'm half crazy all for the love of you.
It won't be a stylish marriage,
I can't afford a carriage.
But you'll look sweet,
Upon the seat,
Of a bicycle made for two.

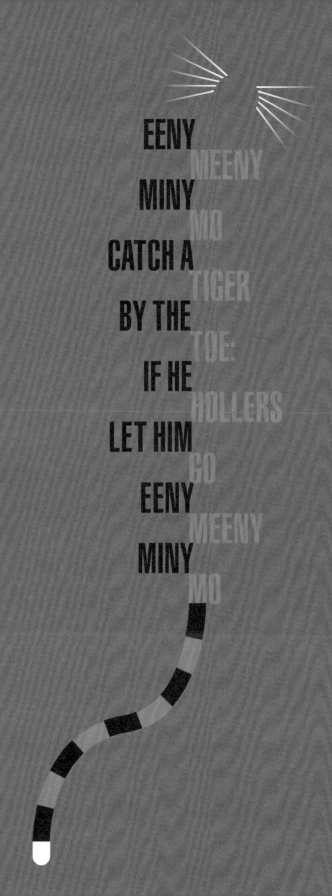

EENY
MEENY
MINY
MO
CATCH A
TIGER
BY THE
TOE:
IF HE
HOLLERS
LET HIM
GO
EENY
MEENY
MINY
MO

A dimple on your cheek, you are gentle and meek.

A dimple on your chin,
you've a devil within.

Hickory dickory dock
The mouse ran up the clock
The clock struck one
The mouse ran down
Hickory dickory dock

A wise old owl
lived in an oak.
The more he saw
the less he spoke.
The less he spoke
the more he heard.
Why can't we all be
like that wise old bird?

There was an old lady who swallowed a cow,
I don't know how she swallowed a cow;
She swallowed the cow to catch the dog,
She swallowed the dog to catch the cat,
She swallowed the cat to catch the bird,
She swallowed the bird to catch the spider,
She swallowed the spider to catch the fly;
I don't know why she swallowed a fly
Perhaps she'll die!

There was an old lady who swallowed
a horse… She's dead, of course.

Old Mr. Match gave
his head a good scratch,
And his face lighted
up with a smile;
"It is getting quite dark,
but with my cheery spark
I will lengthen the day
for awhile."

Little Miss Muffet sat on a tuffet
Eating her curds and whey,
Along came a spider,
Who sat down beside her
And frightened Miss Muffet away

I'd rather have fingers than toes;
I'd rather have ears than a nose;
And as for my hair,
I'm glad it's all there;

I'll be awfully sad, when it goes!

Rain, rain, go away,
Come again another day.
Little Johnny wants to play;
Rain, rain, go to Spain,
Never show your face again!

Pat a cake,
pat a cake,
baker's man
Bake me a cake
as fast as you can.
Pat it and prick it
and mark it with a 'B'
And put it in the oven
for Baby and me.

Humpty Dumpty sat on a wall,
Humpty Dumpty had a great fall.
All the King's horses,
And all the King's men
Couldn't put Humpty together again!

Early in the morning
at eight o'clock
You can hear the
postman's knock;
Up jumps Ella to
answer the door,
One letter, two letters,
three letters, four!

When the snow is on the ground,
Little Robin redbreast grieves.
For no berries can be found,
And on the trees there are no leaves.

The air is cold, the worms are hid.
For this poor bird what can be done?
We'll strew him here some crumbs of bread,
And then he'll live till the snow is gone.

Pease pudding hot
Pease pudding cold
Pease pudding in the pot nine days old
Some like it hot, some like it cold,
Some like it in the pot...

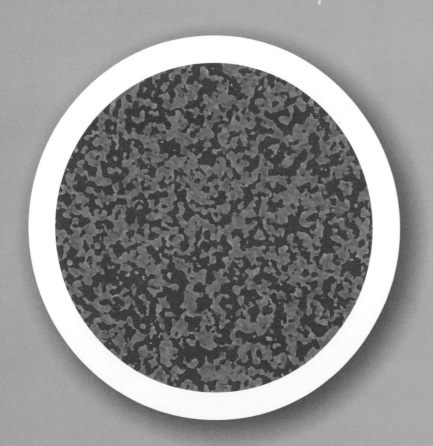

days old

Two little dicky birds

One named Peter,

Fly away Peter,

Come back Peter,

sitting on a wall,

one named Paul.

Baa baa black sheep,
have you any wool?
Yes sir, yes sir,
three bags full!
One for the master,
one for the dame,
And one for the little boy
who lives down the lane.

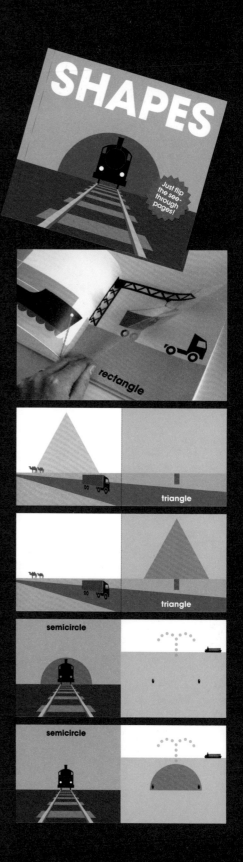